A Country Tale

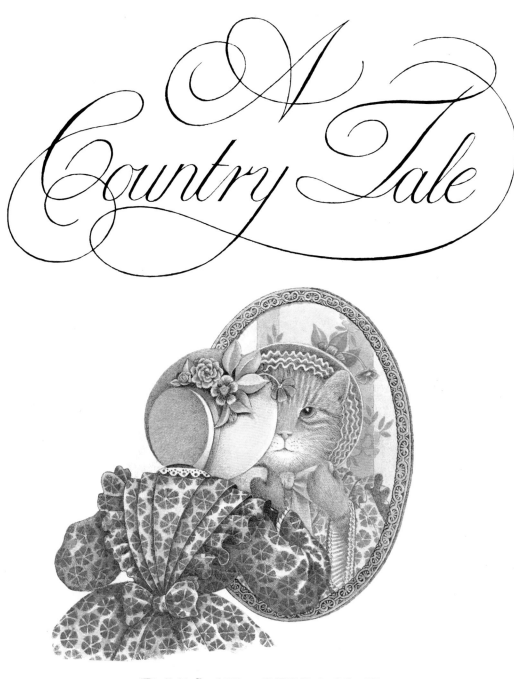

DIANE STANLEY

FOUR WINDS PRESS

MACMILLAN PUBLISHING COMPANY
· NEW YORK ·

COLLIER MACMILLAN PUBLISHERS
· LONDON ·

Macmillan Publishing Company
866 Third Avenue, New York, N.Y. 10022
Collier Macmillan Canada, Inc.

Printed in the United States of America

10   9   8   7   6   5   4   3   2   1

Library of Congress Cataloging in Publication Data

Stanley, Diane.
A country tale.

Summary: An ill-fated visit to the city home of
the elegant Mrs. Snickers teaches an impressionable
country cat a little about herself and friendship.
1. Children's stories, American.   [1. Friendship –
Fiction.   2. Cats – Fiction]   I. Title.
PZ7.S7869Cou 1985   [E]   84-14399
ISBN 0-02-786780-3

FOR
MARINA-BARINA
AND
BABY BOO

leo and Lucy were the warmest of friends. A day rarely passed that one didn't drop by the other's house to bring flowers or borrow a wheelbarrow or ask for some advice. On fine evenings they often climbed Butternut Hill and sat together watching the valley below fade into twilight.

"What did you bake today?" asked Cleo as they climbed the hill one night.

Lucy looked down at the flour on the front of her dress. "Apple pie," she said. "Can't you tell?"

"Yum," said Cleo.

"And not nearly so messy as the raspberry jam," added Lucy.

"For your birthday, I will make you an apron." Cleo giggled, remembering the raspberry jam.

Lucy stopped in her tracks. "What's that?" she asked, pointing up the road.

"It's a lady in a crinoline dress." Cleo straightened her bonnet. "She looks *very* grand."

"Well, she looks *very* uncomfortable to me," said Lucy, trying to brush the flour off her dress.

"Well, it's the very latest thing, I promise you."

The grand lady floated toward them at great speed in spite of her enormous skirts.

"You there! Come here!" she called in a commanding tone.

Cleo and Lucy hurried to meet her.

"I need assistance," the grand lady said. "My carriage is simply *loaded* with baggage and it is stuck halfway up the hill." She sat down on a large rock by the road and began fanning herself. "I will need someone to remove my carriage from its rut so that we may proceed up to the Manse."

"Are you moving into the old Butternut Mansion?" asked Cleo with great interest.

"We will be there for the summer only, of course," she answered, speaking to Cleo. "I am Mrs. Snickers, but my mother was a Butternut, don't you know."

Cleo said that was wonderful.

"Now will you be a dear," said Mrs. Snickers, "and scurry off to find some strong laborers to free my carriage?"

"We'll be glad to," Cleo answered, turning to go.

"No, no, not *you,* my dear. Let the *other* one go." Mrs. Snickers looked sideways at Lucy.

"I'll be as quick as I can," said Lucy softly. She headed down the road.

"*That* one," said Mrs. Snickers, rising and settling herself in a shady spot, "is a bit of a mess, but *you* have possibilities."

The following evening Cleo didn't come by as she usually did, so Lucy watched the sunset alone, wondering.

"I think I'll just go look in on Cleo and make sure everything's all right," she said to herself.

When she reached the gate she saw that Cleo's windows were bare. The lamplight streamed out into the garden.

Lucy opened the front door and saw Cleo sitting in her cozy chair and sewing her curtains into a dress.

"Well, Cleo, what project is this?" asked Lucy.

"I'm making an afternoon dress," said Cleo with a smile.

"Whatever is an afternoon dress?" asked Lucy in astonishment.

"Why, it's a dress with flowers on it, to be worn in the afternoon while drinking tea in the garden under the shade of a large tree...from a silver tea service set on a lace-covered table, of course."

"Oh," said Lucy. "I never do that. I didn't think you did, either."

"Mrs. Snickers does. And so will I when I finish my dress."

"You don't have a lawn *or* a shade tree," said Lucy, "not to mention the tea service or that lace tablecloth."

"But Mrs. Snickers does, and I've been invited to have tea with her every Saturday while she's staying at the Manse. Isn't that exciting?"

Lucy shrugged her shoulders.

"She doesn't wear a bonnet," said Cleo. "Didn't you notice? She wears hats covered with silk flowers and ribbons."

"I suppose you're making a hat, too," Lucy said.

"It will go with the dress," said Cleo.

Lucy got up to leave.

"What are you going to do for curtains?" she asked at the door.

"I think I'll buy velvet ones," said Cleo.

"Does Mrs. Snickers have velvet curtains?" asked Lucy.

"Of course," said Cleo.

At the end of August the Snickers family began packing trunks and boxes for their return to the city. They would attend the opera and theater there, as well as a great number of dances and parties. They would call on their friends for tea and their friends would call on them. The Snickers family had a great many friends.

The last time Cleo had taken tea at the Manse, Mrs. Snickers had said, "You should come see us in town sometime." Mrs. Snickers didn't mention this again, and she left soon after without saying good-by. Even so, Cleo dreamed of going to the city and having tea with Mrs. Snickers and her wonderful friends.

By late September Cleo was tired of everyday life and everyday clothes. When she and Lucy climbed Butternut Hill in the evenings, she forgot to look down on the valley, all pink in the sunset. Instead, she gazed at the Manse and the garden where she had felt so elegant. How she missed dressing up! How she missed Mrs. Snickers! How she missed the silver tea service!

One morning in late September, Cleo rose before dawn. She put on her camisole and her long drawers.

She put on her corset and pulled it so tight she could hardly breathe.

Then she put on four petticoats.

At last she put on her afternoon dress and her hat. She carried a dainty little parasol and a fine needlework bag. She looked in the mirror and made a little pout the way Mrs. Snickers did.

"Perfect!" she said to her reflection. Then she locked her door and set off down the road.

At the edge of the village she met Lucy, picking apples.

"You look grander every time I see you," sighed Lucy as Cleo passed by. "Where are you off to?"

"To visit Mrs. Snickers in the city. She most especially invited me."

"Wait," said Lucy, climbing down the ladder. "I'll walk with you as far as The Famished Bear."

Cleo's skirts stuck out so much that Lucy had to walk on the far side of the road.

"Isn't it hot under all that?" she asked with some amusement.

"Comfort isn't everything," said Cleo, wishing Lucy had stayed at home.

When they reached The Famished Bear, Lucy went inside for a glass of cider and some gossip with the innkeeper.

"I must press on," said Cleo, sounding just like Mrs. Snickers, "or I shall never reach my destination."

"Well, good luck then," sighed Lucy, watching her friend float away in a sea of petticoats.

The city was noisy and crowded. Carriages and wagons filled the streets and jostled bystanders. Beggars stood about in dirty rags looking for anything they could beg or steal.

Cleo walked on quickly until she found the right house on the right street. It was quiet and genteel. She straightened her hat and rang the bell. The butler who answered the door asked for her calling card. Cleo didn't have one. She was asked to wait while the butler went to speak with Mrs. Snickers. It took a long time.

At last she was shown into the parlor where Mrs. Snickers sat, surrounded by bored-looking gentlemen and ladies in silk dresses. Mrs. Snickers introduced Cleo as her "little friend from the country."

"Did you drive in from the country today?" asked one of the ladies.

"No, I walked," said Cleo with a timid smile.

"You *walked!*" shrieked another. "But, my dear, how dreadfully *boring!*"

"Do you keep a city house?" asked the first, doubtfully.

"No, I'm afraid not," apologized Cleo.

"Well, just what do you do?" chimed in a third.

"I farm," said Cleo. "And I sell my needlework."

"Oh," said the lady.

After that no one asked her any more questions. They talked about last night's play and this evening's party. They discussed their friends who weren't there.

Cleo admired the room. She admired the ladies' dresses. She admired the tea service and the cake and the sandwiches. But she was having a terrible time.

"I have to go," said Cleo.

No one seemed to regret it. The butler gave her a mocking smile as he opened the door. She was glad to leave. She hurried through the crowded streets until she came to the road that led to her village.

It was the hottest part of the afternoon. Cleo's back ached. Her feet ached. And deep inside, where her feelings were, her heart ached. She could go no farther.

At the side of the road a great oak tree spread its cool shade above a grassy spot.

"I'll just lie down for a little while," she said to herself, "and then I'll feel better."

Not far away an old thief watched Cleo curl up under the tree and go to sleep.

"Well, just look at those shoes!" she cackled. "Let's trade, shall we, dearie?"

What she left on Cleo's feet could hardly be called shoes, they were so tattered and soiled. For good measure, she took the parasol, too, and hobbled away laughing.

A short time later a beggar child came by, and oh! she wanted that hat! On silent feet she crept up to Cleo, untied the satin ribbon, and slipped it off. She tied her dirty scarf on Cleo's head and scurried off with the hat.

Then an old farmer came along. He was not a beggar or a thief. But he was not as honest as he might have been. He saw Cleo in her shabby shoes and dirty scarf. He saw her fine needlework bag.

"She must have stolen that bag," he told himself. "No reason I shouldn't have it." Now, he had an old basket in which he had carried his wife's eggs to market. In a flash he had exchanged it for Cleo's fine bag.

"That will teach her to steal!" he muttered self-righteously, hurrying away.

Then it began to rain. The dusty road turned to mud. A cart hurried by, drenching Cleo from head to toe. At last she woke up, and what a surprise met her eyes!

Her dress was all brown with mud. Her shoes were rags. Beside her was a decrepit basket. She ran to the road and looked in a puddle. A muddy brown face in a dirty headscarf looked up at her. She had never seen this creature in her life!

"Oh, no!" she cried. "I am not me!"

She looked all around for herself. But all she saw were wet, muddy, tired folk returning from market.

She raced down the road, stopping every now and again to check her reflection, and looking everywhere for her own familiar self. She simply couldn't figure it out, and so she began to cry.

When at last she reached The Famished Bear she saw the innkeeper leaning against the door, smoking a pipe.

"Oh, please sir," she cried, "have you seen an elegant lady in a flowered dress and a fancy hat?"

"Yes, she was here this morning," he said. "Came with Lucy. But she hasn't been back."

"Oh!" said Cleo, and she began to cry even harder.

"Perhaps she's gone home," said the innkeeper, kindly. "Do you know where she lives?"

"Oh, yes, that must be where she is!" cried Cleo.

She arrived at her village as the sun was setting. Lucy was leaning on her garden wall, watching the sky change colors.

"Oh, Lucy," cried Cleo, "the most dreadful thing has happened! I have turned into somebody else!"

Lucy began to laugh. "How did it happen?" she asked.

"I fell asleep by the roadside. When I woke up I wasn't there. Oh, what shall I do?"

"Let's go look at Cleo's house," said Lucy with a smile. She took Cleo's arm and led her along.

"That's the house," said Cleo.

"I know," said Lucy. "See if you have a key in your pocket that unlocks the door."

She did.

Then she saw her reflection in the mirror. "Cleo's not here either," she sobbed.

"Why don't you just take off that dress," suggested Lucy, "and put on Cleo's everyday one. I'm sure she wouldn't mind."

"Well, I suppose so," said Cleo, "until the mud is washed off."

"And here are Cleo's slippers," said Lucy. "Cleo would want you to wear them."

"If you really think so...," said Cleo.

"Here, wash your face and hands. Cleo would suggest it if she were here."

"Cleo is very hospitable," said Cleo, washing away the mud.

"Oh, look!" said Lucy, pointing to the mirror. "There she is!"

"Where, where?" cried Cleo, running to see. When she saw her reflection in the mirror, she cried with joy.

"It's me! I'm back!"

"And *thank goodness*!" said Lucy with a grin.

So they had supper together and listened to the crickets chirp.

"I had a terrible time," said Cleo.

"I thought you might," said Lucy. "Have some apple pie."

And they sat together until very late, watching the stars come out.